JESSICA SOUHAMI

studied at the Central School of Art and Design. In 1980 she

formed Mme Souhami and Co., a travelling puppet company using

colourful shadow puppets with a musical accompaniment and a storyteller.

Her books for Frances Lincoln are just as vibrant and funny as her puppet shows.

They include **The Leopard's Drum**, **Rama and the Demon King**, **No Dinner!**,

In the Dark, Dark Wood, **Mrs McCool and the Giant Cúchulainn**,

The Famous Adventure of a Bird-Brained Hen and **The Little, Little House**.

SAUSAGES

Jessica Souhami

F

FRANCES LINCOLN
CHILDREN'S BOOKS

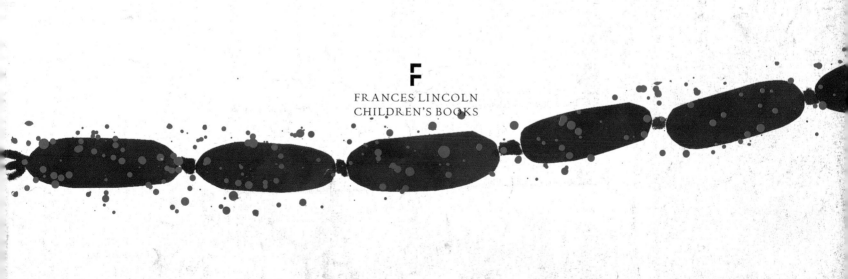

Sausages is Jessica Souhami's version of a famous story called **The Three Wishes** which can be traced back to Ancient India and Ancient Greece. The first popular version was published in France in the 17th century, but a little-known version from 12th-century Britain also exists. The story most of us know derives from the tale collected by the Grimm brothers in the 19th century.

First published in Great Britain and the USA in 2006 by
Frances Lincoln Children's Books, 4 Torriano Mews,
Torriano Avenue, London NW5 2RZ
www.franceslincoln.com

First paperback edition published in Great Britain in 2007

British Library Cataloguing in Publication Data available on request

ISBN 978-1-84507-601-6

Illustrated with collages of Ingres paper hand-painted with watercolour inks and graphite pencil

Set in HelveticaNeue

Printed in China

9 8 7 6 5 4 3 2 1

One day, a poor woodcutter called John found an elf
stuck on a rose thorn.
"Poor little thing!" said John, and gently lifted the elf free.

"Thank you," said the elf. "In return for your kindness,
I grant you three magic wishes."
He shook out his wings and flew away, calling back,
"Be careful what you wish for!"

And he was gone.

John rushed home to tell his wife the good news.

"Dear Martha," he said, "we shall be rich for the rest of our lives. We must sit down, think hard, and choose our three wishes very carefully."

So John and Martha sat by the fire
and thought and thought, and thought again,
of all the lovely things they could wish for.

But it was difficult to choose.
They sighed, and thought some more.

After several hours, John felt his tummy rumbling.
It would not stop.

"I'm starving, Martha," he said.
"I wish we had some sausages."

And...

...with a **WH...OOO...SH,**
out from the chimney shot a string of sizzling, succulent sausages!

Martha and John stared at the sausages –

and they stared at each other.

"You foolish man!" cried Martha.
"You've wasted a whole wish.

Just think of all the grand things
we could have chosen with that wish.

And all we've got is sausages!

I wish these silly sausages were stuck
to the end of your nose!"

And guess what ...?

Yes! WH...OOO...SH!

The sausages leapt on to the end of John's nose,
where they stuck fast.

Two wishes gone and nothing but sausages.
And they were on John's nose!

Now John was angry.

"For goodness' sake, Martha," he cried,
"get these things off my nose!"

and she

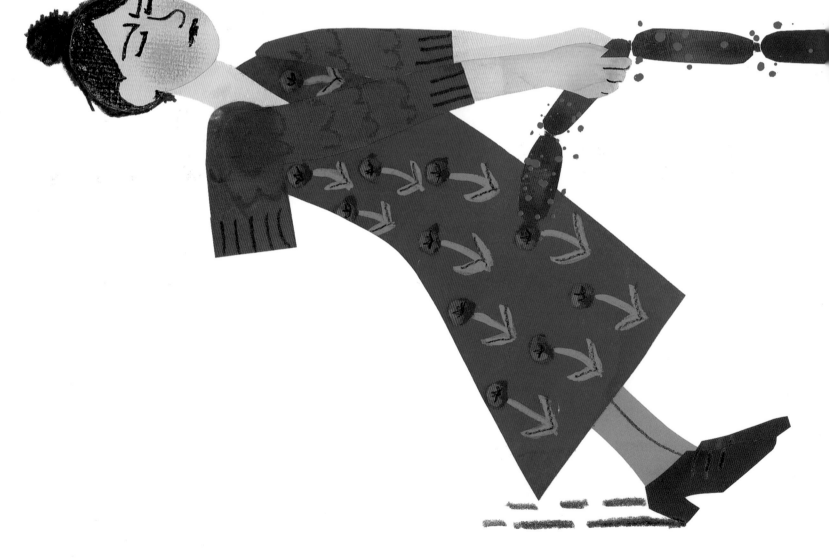

pulled...

and she tugged...

but she could not pull the sausages

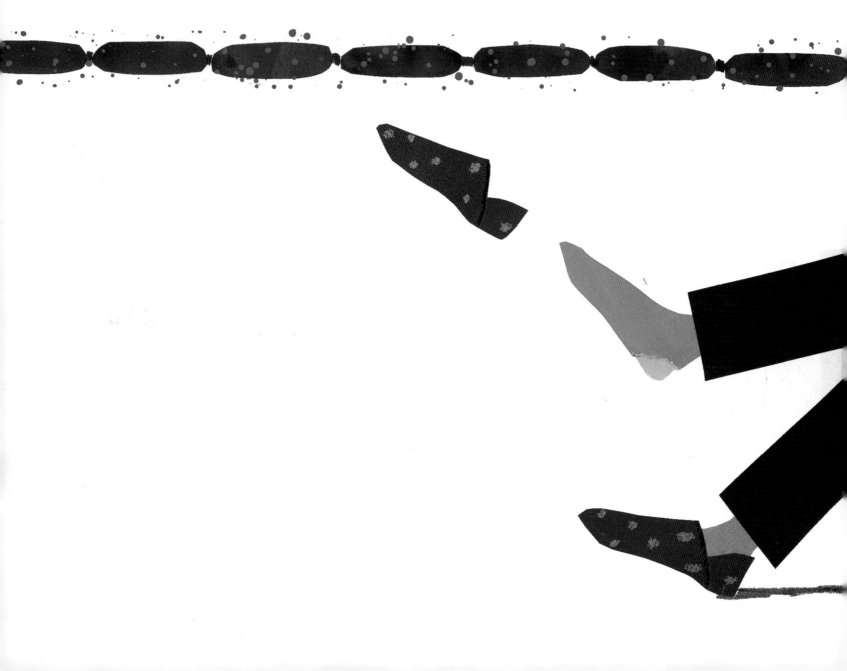

off the end of John's nose.

So she let go and...

John fell on the floor with a bump.

"Oh, by poor, poor dose," he said. "Id's so sore!"

"My dear husband," cried Martha, feeling sorry for John.
"We've been through good times and bad times together.
It's silly for stupid wishes to make us cross."

She took a deep breath.
"I wish these sausages would fall off John's nose."

And **WH...OOOOO**

OO...SH, they did.

John gave Martha a big hug.
"Well, my dear, we've lost our chance to be rich.

But we have each other – and a very good dinner!"

And far away, a little elf laughed.

OTHER PICTURE BOOKS BY JESSICA SOUHAMI FROM FRANCES LINCOLN CHILDREN'S BOOKS

The Famous Adventure of a Bird-Brained Hen

Henny Penny was so bird-brained that when an acorn fell, BOP! on her head,
she thought the sky must be falling. She set out at once to tell the king,
collecting her silly friends along the way. But Foxy Loxy was always just ahead
and he was HUNGRY. So did Henny Penny get to see the king?
And did Foxy Loxy eat a good dinner that night?

ISBN 978-0-7112-2026-3 (UK)
ISBN 978-1-84507-263-6 (US)

The Leopard's Drum

Osebo the leopard has a fine, a huge, a magnificent drum, but he won't
let anyone else have it – not even Nyame the Sky-god. So Nyame
offers a big reward to the animal who will bring him the drum…
How a very small tortoise outwits the boastful leopard is retold
by Jessica Souhami in this traditional tale from West Africa.

ISBN 978-1-84507-506-4

Rama and the Demon King

This is the story of the brave and good prince Rama and his battle
against Ravana, the evil ten-headed king of all the demons.

ISBN 978-0-7112-1158-2 (UK)
ISBN 978-1-84507-361-9 (US)

Frances Lincoln titles are available from all good bookshops.
You can also buy books and find out more about your favourite titles,
authors and illustrators at our website: www.franceslincoln.com